What They're Saying

"A necessary, blistering examination of race and identity that hits with the force of a gut punch... This is a book I'll be recommending widely — it's raw, real, and essential."
— Paul Zietsman, Readers' Favorite ★★★★★

"FUCK THAT is a raw, uncompromising work about mixed-race identity that refuses to comfort or educate."
— IndieReader Staff ★★★★★

"Brutally honest, beautifully crafted... a voice that doesn't just deserve to be heard — it demands it."
— Jamie Michele, Readers' Favorite ★★★★★

"Blistering in its clarity... Ericson's prose alternates between measured analysis and controlled detonation."
— Edward Sung, IndieReader ★★★★★

Also by Joshua Ericson

Books Available Now

Think, Rethink, Panic: How to Survive Your Own Brain (Barely)

Fuck That: A Fictional Memoir

Coming Soon

Antisocial (October 2025)

Therapy is Weird: Apparently I'm the Problem (2026)

Fine. Whatever. : A Marriage Story (TBD)

Good Enough: *Becoming a Perfection-ish Parent (TBD)*

What Was I Doing? *A Field Guide to ADHD Chaos (TBD)*

A Week in the Life (TBD)

Fuck That

A Fictional Memoir

JOSHUA ERICSON

Fuck That: A Fictional Memoir by Joshua Ericson

Copyright © 2025 by Joshua Ericson

First printing, 2025

This is a work of fiction. Names, characters, places, and events are products of the author's imagination or are used fictitiously. Any resemblance to actual persons, living or dead, or actual events is purely coincidental.

ISBN: 979-8-9929431-4-6
ASIN: B0FDTHGLZ8

First edition: August 2025

All rights reserved. No part of this publication may be reproduced, distributed, or transmitted in any form or by any means, including photocopying, recording, or other electronic or mechanical methods, without the prior written permission of the publisher, except in cases permitted by U.S. copyright law and for the use of quotations in a book review.

This book contains mature themes and subject matter, and depictions of violence. Reader discretion is advised.

Book design by Joshua Ericson
Cover design by Joshua Ericson

Published by
Brain vs Me Publishing
www.brainvsme.com

"There's a point where adaptation becomes erasure."

Chapter One

Nah

I'm not here to make you comfortable.

I am not your assumption, your checkbox, or your story to tell.

I am not Black. I am not white. I am not the color of my skin.

I am not a stereotype.

I am not your goddamn checkbox.

I do not exist to validate your quota. I do not exist to make you feel like an ally. I do not exist to make you feel better about yourself. I am not here to teach you how to treat people with basic decency. I am not here to help you become more tolerant. I am not here to ask for your pity on behalf of an entire race.

I will never be what you want me to be.

I am me.

And if that annoys you, good.

If you want me to quiet down?

Fuck that.

One of my favorite guilty-pleasure movies from the 2000s is Wanted, the 2008 one (James McAvoy, Angelina Jolie, Morgan Freeman). There's this moment about halfway through the movie where McAvoy's character snaps. Everyone's pressuring him, shaping him, breaking him down, and he yells: "I don't know who I am."

That line? That's been mine since I was old enough to hear my own silence.

I've worn masks my whole life. Some I built to survive. Some I wore just to belong. But one mask, one mask was thrust upon me without consent.

Scientifically speaking, I'm mixed race. White mother. Black father. Both American. One present. One not. One who raised me. One who didn't get a chance.

My father was never with my mother, not really. He was married to someone else, still wanted the chance to raise me, but was denied. We left when I was five or six. My mother was running. She moved me to a place with an unlisted phone number, the middle of nowhere, and cut off from everything I knew.

She raised me in a tiny town on the East Coast, three thousand people, give or take. All white.

My school: white.
My church: white.
My friends, my girlfriends, my reflection: split.

I was the only Black kid I knew until tenth grade. And yet, I wasn't bullied. Not really.

I always assumed it was because I wasn't a threat. Just one of me. Just me.

I told myself I wasn't Black. I wasn't white. I was just... trying.

And then I graduated. Left the bubble. Stepped out into a world that didn't ask questions; it dictated. It saw me. Saw what I'd survived. Shrugged. Told me that none of that mattered. Only one thing did: the color of my skin.

So they gave me the mask. Attached the label with a pin, drew blood. Handed me the weight of twenty generations. Pushed me down and said: "Good luck."

Which didn't mean good luck.

It meant what someone told me not long after I graduated and stepped into the wrong restaurant, at the wrong time, in front of the wrong person.

It was a welcome I will never forget: "Know your place, n*****."

I didn't stay long. Not in that physical place. Not in my mental place. I was lost. Alone... and absolutely unprepared and unequipped to deal with my new reality. I had no shelter. No safe zone.

I had to grow up quickly.

I confided in the few people I trusted. People that love to say, "Be proud of who you are." And I am.

But who I am isn't a race.

Who I am is a person, someone who grew up in whiteness, shaped by absence, and still dared to learn, to grow, to name what others refused to see.

Despite the grades, the degrees, the diction. Despite being quiet when I was told. Loud when I had to be. Despite knowing White America better than it knows itself.

I've spent my life in a system designed to erase me. Shrink me. Slap a label on me and shove me in a box with no air holes.

The world tells me all I am is Black. That's all they choose to see. And to that, I say:
Fuck that.

I had a good education. I was raised to be kind. To be strong. To think for myself. The world didn't care. The world said that wasn't enough. Said I was Black, and that was that. So I was supposed to conform. Supposed to act a certain way. Speak a certain way. Live a certain way. Die a certain way.

Fuck that.

I'm a Black man raised in a white world. But I've always been too Black for White America and too white for Black America. I don't get to pick a side. A side was picked for me.

And in a way, I'm glad. Because I will always stand with the oppressed, even when the oppressed don't stand with me.

I'm done asking for acceptance. I don't need it.

I don't need permission. I just need a megaphone.

I am me. I'm good enough.

And I know you want me to shut up.

To quiet down. To go back in the box you built for me.

Fuck that.

That box is a coffin. And I'm done being buried.

I don't like what I like because of a label. I like what I like because I have a mind.

I know what I know because I went out and learned it.

I will make my own way.

No matter what you say.

No matter what you do.

Fuck that.

I know my place. I do not care.

I know the consequences. I do not care.

I know I'd be better off keeping my mouth shut.

Fuck that.

Chapter Two

The First Cut

The office was still, quiet like a trap.

High floor. Glass walls. The hum of the HVAC overhead pretending to be silence. I sat behind the desk they gave me, suit jacket draped over the back of my chair, sleeves rolled. Laptop open, untouched. Cursor blinking like a dare.

I wasn't working. I was stewing.

That morning, my boss asked if I'd consider leading our company's Diversity & Inclusion initiative.

"Asked" is generous. It was framed as an opportunity, a compliment, a chance to make an impact. "We think you'd bring a unique perspective," he'd said, his smile all polished intent. "Your voice really matters right now."

I knew what he meant. I've always known.

You mean I'm Black. Just say it.

And maybe that would've stung less if it weren't always the same script. The same invitation. The same leash. I've never been allowed to just do the job I was hired for. There's always some side quest, some optics gig, some corporate reckoning I'm supposed to shepherd, for their healing, not mine.

I stared at the screen, my reflection faint in the glass.

I've worn masks my whole life. Some for protection. Some for survival. But this one, this mask?

This one was handed to me, without consent.

The conference room was fluorescent-bright and beige with ambition.

That kind of neutral, corporate optimism, ceiling tiles humming, fake wood table gleaming like it had something to prove.

David Langley sat at the head. Crisp button-down. Rolled-up sleeves. The picture of progressive white leadership. The kind of man who reads Ibram X. Kendi on a plane and quotes it in meetings like scripture. The kind who thinks eye contact is a substitute for accountability.

He leaned forward like he was about to share a secret.

"We've been thinking," he said. "There's a real need for someone to take the lead on our division's D&I efforts. And we think you'd be perfect."

Perfect.

Because I check the box.

Because I speak the language.

Because I can talk about race without making white people cry.

I nodded. Smiled. Said, "Of course. I'd be honored."

Auto-pilot.

Internally, something cracked. Not a clean break, not yet. But a fracture. A sharp little tremor behind the ribs. And I felt it. Not just in my body, in the room.

Because this time, it didn't feel like recognition. It felt like recruitment. Like conscription.

Like they were calling in a debt I never agreed to owe. A favor owed to them, not for my skill, but for my presence.

My utility.

My Blackness, leveraged.

David smiled like we'd made history together. Reached under the table and handed me a glossy folder, our newest Diversity & Inclusion Statement. Hot off the printer.

I opened it. Read the first line.

"We stand together."

Of course you do.

I flipped to the next paragraph. "We're committed to listening, to learning, to healing as a community."

Healing from what? From whom?

It read like a eulogy for George Floyd, edited by Legal and approved by Branding.

It read like what white guilt sounds like when it's had media training.

I nodded again. Took the packet. Said nothing.

Walked out before the bile could reach my throat.

Down the hallway. Past the framed stock photos of smiling teams. Past the mission statement etched in glass. Past the values we only performed when someone was watching.

And when I got back to my desk, I sat still for a long time. Hands in my lap. The folder on the corner of my keyboard like a dare.

And all I could think was:

This isn't a promotion.

This is a script.

And they just cast me to make the story sound better.

Back at my desk, I pulled up the leadership roster. Photo grid. Corporate headshots. Smiling faces with perfect lighting. Title after title: VP. SVP. EVP. All the acronyms of authority.

I counted.

Forty-eight faces. Forty-four white. Four "diverse." Two Black. One South Asian. One ambiguously brown enough to be used in every brochure.

No executives. No real power. Just proximity.

I moved to the Board of Directors. Different page. Same pattern.

One woman of color, framed like a trophy.

They wanted me to stand in front of this.

To explain it.

To defend it.

To "reassure the workforce" that progress was being made, that our values were real, that our equity work was working.

But what they really wanted was something else.

A face.

A voice.

A translator.

"You want me to lead the parade for your optics," I muttered, jaw tight. "You want me to make your problem look like progress."

You want my skin to cover your statistics.

You want my tone to make the data sound like a story worth clapping for.

I closed the tab.

Sat back. Hands flat on the desk. Breath low and even.

Then I opened the page again.

Just to look. Just to stare. Just to let the rage build in my chest. Not chaos. Not fury. Not fire and glass and broken furniture.

No.

This was precision rage. The kind that doesn't scream.

It sharpens.

It watches.

It memorizes names.

It remembers who smiled and said "thank you for your leadership" while doing nothing at all.

It studies the grid, not with despair, but with clarity. This isn't a pipeline problem. This is a preference problem. This is a comfort problem. This is what happens when whiteness hires itself and calls it merit.

I looked at my own photo. Same corporate crop. Same strained smile. Staring out from the bottom corner of the org chart like a reluctant mascot.

I closed the tab one last time. And whispered, not loud but loud enough for me to hear: "I'm not your goddamn solution."

First grade. Winter.

The desks were pushed into a horseshoe, like we were supposed to be having a conversation instead of being measured.

The radiator clicked in the corner. Chalkdust floated in a shaft of pale light near the board. I remember the sound my snow boots made against the tile, rubber squeaking, snow melting into a puddle that made the kid next to me scoot his chair an inch away.

I sat near the back. Not because I liked it there, but because that's where they put me.

We were reading aloud. One paragraph at a time. Left to right, clockwise, like passing a baton.

When it got to me, I read smooth. No stumbles. Clear voice. Full stops. I had practiced. I always practiced.

Halfway through my paragraph, a boy, maybe Kyle, maybe Ethan, leaned toward the kid next to him and whispered something.

I didn't hear it at first. Just noticed the kid next to him make a face, like surprise mixed with confusion. Then I heard it again.

"The Black kid reads good."

Not loud. But not quiet enough to stay secret.

I didn't flinch. Just kept reading. Eyes on the page. Words clean.

But something in me shifted.

Because I didn't know what it meant, not exactly. But I knew it wasn't a compliment.

It was said like a discovery.

Like I was an exception. A surprise.

Like I was a contradiction.

That's what landed in my chest.

That I'd done something unexpected just by doing what I was supposed to do.

That was the first time I realized I was being watched, not as a person, but as a category.

Not "Michael."

Just "The Black kid."

A specimen.

And the worst part?

The teacher didn't say anything.

She'd heard it. I saw her pause.

But she didn't correct him.

Didn't affirm me.

Didn't name it.

She let it float there. Unchallenged. Unspoken.

Like it was just one of those things kids say.

Like it wasn't the beginning of something sharp and permanent.

After class, I didn't tell anyone. I didn't go home and cry. I didn't even understand what had happened, not fully.

But something lodged in my spine that day. A small, hard truth I'd carry for years before I had the words for it.

Being good at something wasn't just about being good.

It was about being good despite.

Despite the color of my skin.

Despite the story they'd already written for me.

I wasn't seen.

I was scanned.

And that day, I learned: You don't have to be hated to be dehumanized.

Sometimes, all it takes is being surprised that I can read.

Back in the glass cage, the light had changed. The city outside was dark now, blinking and busy.

I closed the laptop. Took a deep breath.

"I've spent my life being what makes other people comfortable."

My voice was steady. I said it aloud, just once, to the room.

"Not anymore."

I didn't know who I was. Not yet. But I knew what I wasn't. I wasn't their face. I wasn't their Black box, checked and compliant. I wasn't their photo op.

I turned off the light. And walked out.

Chapter Three

One of One

The town had three thousand people, maybe.

Wooded, religious, political; the kind of place that called itself neutral, but whiteness was in the water, passed down like well water and last names. I didn't know that then. I just knew the roads were long, the mailboxes were far apart, and everyone waved from their porch like you were expected to wave back.

To me, it was normal. I didn't know there was a different kind of normal.

We moved there when I was five, after my mother cut my father out for good. It was supposed to be safer, quieter. A place where no one would ask about bruises or bloodlines. But that silence had a cost.

My school was white. My friends were white. The church we went to: white. Every girlfriend I had, every birthday party I got invited to, every goddamn photograph on the wall: white.

I was the only Black kid I knew until tenth grade.

And somehow, I wasn't bullied. Not in the way people expect. No fights. No beatings. Just the slow erosion of invisibility. The kind that doesn't hit you in the face; it wears you down quietly, like rust.

Looking back, I think it's because I wasn't a threat. Just one of me. Just me. The polite kid. The smart one. The one who knew how to laugh at the right jokes and nod at the right time. I was palatable.

I wore whiteness like a hand-me-down coat. It never fit right, but I learned not to complain.

Because different was dangerous.

And I didn't know yet that the cost of safety was self-erasure.

It was third grade when I learned my body could betray me.

Mrs. Anderson was the gym teacher. Mid-forties, bowl cut, tracksuit; the kind of woman who always seemed slightly out of breath, even when standing still. She had a whistle she didn't need and a smile that never reached her eyes.

That day, we were learning about speed. Or power. Or something physical that could've stayed theoretical.

She asked me to stand up.

I didn't know why at first. I just followed instructions, like always. That's what you do when you're the only one: you don't ask questions, you just obey.

She had the whole class gather around. Then she pointed to my legs. My glutes. Told them to look. Said this (my anatomy) was why Black people ran faster. Said it like a compliment. Like science.

I didn't move. Didn't speak. I just stood there, a human diagram.

She said it like a lesson. Like she was educating them. Like my ass was her visual aid. She didn't see what she was doing, or maybe she did, and she saw a chance to sound scientific, to turn me into curriculum.

There was a moment (not long, maybe five seconds) where everything inside me froze. I wasn't a kid anymore. I was a specimen. A Black body being explained to a room full of white kids by a white woman in a polyester tracksuit.

I remember my skin prickling. My ears hot. My eyes focused on the basketball net above the stage. I stared at it like it was going to save me. It didn't.

The kids laughed. I didn't. Not until after. That's when the teasing started. And when one kid said too much, I hit him. I was nine. They acted like I was supposed to take it forever.

That was the first time I felt shame I couldn't name.

I didn't tell anyone. Not my mom. Not my grandmother. Not even myself, not really. I buried it. Because what would I have said?

How do you explain that you were humiliated without violence?

That someone weaponized your body without touching it?

Back then, I didn't have the words. I just knew something shifted. Some curtain lifted. And behind it was this truth I wasn't ready for:

They already saw me a certain way, long before I ever understood what it meant.

After that, I started noticing the other comments. The way teachers would talk about my "natural athleticism." The way classmates would joke that I must be fast, or strong, or "built for sports." As if Blackness came with a starter pack.

But I wasn't fast. I wasn't built. I was quiet. Skinny. Bookish. I liked reading and drawing and figuring things out. But none of that mattered. Because they'd already filled in the blanks.

The gym teacher didn't know it, but she started something that day.

She gave my difference a name, even if I wasn't allowed to say it.

And from then on, every room I walked into already had a script written.

I was just learning how to play the part.

I started asking about my father when I was eight.

It wasn't defiance. It was hunger, a kind of ache. I wanted to know who I came from, what he looked like, why no one ever said his name. There was a gap in me, and I thought maybe if I could just fill it with a story, even a bad one, I could stop feeling so split.

My mother tried to brush it off at first. "He wasn't around much," she'd say, folding laundry like the conversation was just another chore. "You're better off."

But I kept asking. I needed more than that. I wanted details. I wanted proof I hadn't been dropped into this world by accident.

One day, I pushed too hard. I don't even remember what I said; maybe something about wanting to meet him, or why he never called. But she snapped.

And just like that, the door opened. Not gently. Violently.

She told me everything. The hospital they worked at. The short, failed thing that passed for dating. The fact that he was already married. The fact that I was a secret. The fact that she wasn't sure she wanted me at first. The fact that when she decided to keep me, she'd tried to protect me, and herself, by leaving.

Then she told me the part I never asked for: the part about how I was conceived.

I won't write the details here. Just know this: I learned, at eight years old, that I was not made from love. I was not planned. I was not even wanted, not really.

My grandmother didn't say much during any of this. She just sat at the kitchen table, clutching her tea like a prop. Her silence wasn't passive. It had weight. It had teeth. She never said she resented me, but I felt it. In her eyes. In the way her lips pressed together whenever the subject came up, or didn't.

I knew he was a bad man. I knew the story. But I still wanted to know him. I wanted to know he was real. I wanted someone who looked like me to explain the other half of my face. The other half of my blood. I didn't want love. I wanted a witness. I wanted a map.

But after that, I stopped asking.

It wasn't that I had answers now; it was that the questions had become radioactive. Dangerous to carry.

I tried to bring up race once. Not even in an accusatory way. I was maybe ten or eleven. I said something like, "Everyone sees me as Black."

My mother looked up from the sink and said, without turning off the water, "But I don't."

That was it.

No discussion. No curiosity. Just a white woman's love trying to overwrite a Black child's reality.

I learned the rules early: You don't talk about the father. You don't talk about race. You don't talk about what doesn't fit.

Our house wasn't abusive. It was quiet. Too quiet. And in that silence, the shame grew roots.

If I wanted to keep the peace, I had to keep the questions inside.

So I did.

I buried them where they'd grow wild and tangled; and no one else would have to see.

It happened at the kitchen table. We weren't fighting. We weren't even talking about anything serious. It was just one of those after-dinner moments: the kind where plates sit in the sink and the air smells like whatever was cooked too long. I was maybe eleven or twelve, still trying to find the shape of things.

I said it like a fact: "People make fun of me because I'm Black."

I wasn't looking for a debate. I wasn't angry. I just needed someone to say, Yeah, I see it too. You're not imagining it. You're not alone in it.

My mother didn't even pause.

She said, "I don't even see you as Black."

Her voice was gentle. Maybe even proud. Like she was giving me a compliment. A gift.

But what I heard was this: I don't see the part of you the world fears. The part it targets. The part that gets pulled over, passed over, pointed at. I don't see the part of you that you're learning to hate.

She meant well. That was the worst part.

She loved me. She raised me. She worked two jobs and fought for a better life for us. But love doesn't cancel blindness. And blindness doesn't erase the bruise.

Her version of safety was denial.

And in that moment, I knew: she would never understand what it meant to walk through the world in this skin. Because she didn't have to.

She could choose not to see it. I didn't get that luxury.

I nodded. Didn't say anything. Let the silence sit where the rest of me wasn't welcome.

From then on, race lived in the walls of our house: silent, present, unacknowledged.

We didn't talk about what the neighbors whispered. We didn't talk about why certain doors didn't open. We didn't talk about what it meant to be the only one in the school picture who looked like me.

And I learned something dangerous from that silence.

I learned to doubt my own experience.

I learned that if my mother didn't see my Blackness, then maybe it wasn't real.

Maybe the discomfort I felt in classrooms and grocery stores and locker rooms was just in my head.

Maybe the stares were misread.

Maybe the shame belonged to me, not the world.

I know better now.

But back then? I needed her to look me in the eye and say, I see you. All of you.

Instead, she gave me erasure dressed as love.

And I carried that silence for years: thinking it was safety, thinking it was protection, thinking it was enough.

It wasn't.

Chapter Four

The Rehearsal

Midday. Spring semester. Sunlight coming through the tall glass windows, hitting the shelves in that lazy, golden way that makes everything feel safe. I was eighteen.

There was a girl (white, like everyone else in my world) who worked the counter. We'd talked before. Smiles. Jokes. Nothing heavy. She had this easy way about her, like she didn't need to try too hard to be liked. And for a minute, standing there, we were just two students talking about something meaningless: a book, maybe, or music, or what classes sucked the most.

And then she said it. Casual. Offhanded. Like she was just pointing out the weather.

"You look like you're from the city, but you sound like you're from the country."

I laughed. I always laughed. But inside, something folded in half and stayed there.

It wasn't violent. Wasn't even meant to be cruel. But it was the first time I realized, really realized, that the world saw me before it heard me. That no matter how I spoke, how polite I was, how many shared references I'd memorized, it didn't matter.

I had a look. A label. A category I didn't choose.

My skin walked into the room first. And nothing else I carried (my voice, my upbringing, my confusion) could outrun it.

She didn't mean anything by it. I know that.

That's what made it worse.

That sentence was a mirror. Twelve words that showed me how invisible I'd been all along, or maybe how clearly I'd been seen, just not in the way I wanted.

I left the store not angry. Just gutted.

I never talked to her again.

Not because I hated her, but because I couldn't bear to be that exposed again: smiling while bleeding out internally, making jokes while my identity splintered under the weight of someone else's perception.

After that moment, everything shifted.

I started cataloging. Every time someone looked at me too long. Every time they said I "spoke well." Every time they seemed surprised I listened to rock or used big words or didn't sag my pants. Things I'd brushed off for years suddenly had shape, texture, weight.

This wasn't about preference. It was about presumption.

That one comment cracked open every other comment. Every other moment I'd minimized. Every other silence I'd swallowed.

That was the day I started to wonder if who I thought I was...was even visible to anyone else.

It didn't matter that I was raised around white people. That I liked the same shows, wore the same clothes, passed every damn test.

I looked like something else. And that something came with its own script.

And apparently, I'd been performing the wrong role.

I didn't tell anyone what she said. Not my friends. Not my mom. Not even myself, not in the way that mattered. I just stopped going to the bookstore. Found new places to kill time between classes. Kept moving.

But something stayed stuck. A knot I couldn't untie.

I started watching myself. Listening to my own voice like it belonged to someone else. Noticing the way I enunciated, the way I walked, the way I responded when someone threw a joke my way that leaned too hard on race.

Was I code-switching? Was I trying too hard?

I didn't have those words then. Just a growing discomfort in my skin, like a shirt I'd worn all my life suddenly didn't fit.

I used to speak without thinking. Now I rehearsed. Rewrote. Trimmed the parts that sounded "too smart," "too square." I'd study other Black students on campus: the way they moved, how they dressed, what they listened to. I wasn't stalking them. I was trying to learn.

Not out of curiosity, but out of desperation.

Because in that one sentence, "You look like you're from the city, but you sound like you're from the country," I realized I was being read like a contradiction. Like a glitch in the matrix.

I didn't know where I belonged anymore.

Too Black to be white. Too white to be Black. I'd heard that phrase before; always shrugged it off. But now it felt like a diagnosis. Like something I couldn't unhear.

I started adjusting. Quietly. Strategically.

Downloaded more hip-hop. Practiced the slang. Changed the way I dressed (nothing extreme, just little things). Different sneakers. A hoodie here, a chain there. I wanted to belong to something. To someone. To a version of me that felt real and rooted.

But every change felt like a costume. A guess.

Like I was playing catch-up to a culture I was supposed to inherit, but had been raised too far away from to claim.

I began to feel shame. Deep, corrosive shame. Not for being mixed. Not for being raised white. But for the fact that I had no idea what I was doing, and that I felt like I had to do anything at all.

There were moments in the dining hall or the dorm lobby where I'd catch someone looking at me, another Black student, and I'd wonder what they saw. Could they tell I was faking it? Could they smell the suburb on me? The whiteness in my vowels?

The truth is, I was grieving something I'd never been given.

A language. A rhythm. A history that was supposed to be mine, but felt foreign. Locked behind a door I didn't have the key to.

It wasn't just a crisis of race. It was a crisis of self.

I didn't know where the mask ended and the person began. Didn't know if I was faking it, or finally trying to be who I was always meant to be.

What I did know was this: the world didn't care about my background. It didn't care how I was raised. It saw the skin. And filled in the rest.

After the bookstore moment, I didn't just reevaluate how I was seen, I reevaluated how I saw myself.

I wanted to be "more Black." Whatever that meant. I didn't have a map for it. Just a deep, rising urgency to be something that felt closer to what the world expected, and what I had never been taught.

So I studied.

Music came first. Out went the alternative rock and acoustic singer-songwriters. In came Tupac, Nas, Biggie, then Kendrick, Cole, Mos Def. I didn't just listen. I analyzed. Read Genius annotations. Memorized lines. Tried to find myself in the anger and the rhythm and the clarity. Sometimes I did. Sometimes I didn't.

Next came the speech.

I listened more than I talked. Picked up new phrases, let them roll around in my mouth before trying them out. Dropped contractions into my sentences. Softened my consonants. Practiced casual. Practiced cool.

It felt like learning a second language, except it was one everyone assumed I already knew.

Then the clothes.

I stopped wearing polos and neutral khakis. Bought a couple graphic tees, some Jordans, a hoodie with a clean logo. Not flashy. Just adjusted. Enough to signal proximity. To suggest a culture I wasn't born into but was tired of being exiled from.

I watched other Black students, how they moved, laughed, nodded to each other like they spoke the same unspoken thing. I wanted that. Not to mimic, but to connect.

But it never quite landed.

There was always this split-second hesitation, a pause before the handshake, a raised eyebrow, a too-long glance. Nothing hostile. Just a quiet audit I never seemed to pass.

One guy in class (deep voice, natural confidence) once said to me, "You cool, but you different."

I laughed, but it stuck with me for weeks.

What did different mean? And why did it feel like a polite way of saying "not enough"?

White people assumed I was Black. Black people weren't sure.

And I floated between, like a student trying to ace a test with no textbook and no teacher, just a list of expectations no one would hand me.

I started performing harder. Not loud. Not obnoxious. Just sharper. More aware of every word, every nod, every beat I let drop into conversation. I wanted to be fluent. Not to impress, but to finally feel like I was speaking something true.

But it always felt rehearsed.

Like I was acting in a play where everyone else had lived the lines and I was just trying not to miss my cues.

I wanted to be claimed.

But the truth was, I didn't even know who I was asking for permission from.

And worse, I wasn't sure they'd give it.

Chapter Five

Not Black Enough, Never White

N o one ever said it directly. Not at first.

It was in the pauses. The side-eyes. The too-loud laughs when I joined the table and tried to keep up. I was sixteen, maybe seventeen, finally in a school with more than two Black kids. And I wanted in.

The lunchroom had its invisible borders: White tables, Black tables, athlete tables, weird kid tables. The Black table was loud. Confident. Unapologetic. The kind of energy that moved without asking for permission.

I didn't belong anywhere else, so I hovered. Tried to blend in. Pulled up a chair like I'd earned it.

They didn't kick me out. They just let me feel how unwelcome I was.

"Why you talk like that?"

"You sound like a teacher."

"You don't even listen to real music."

It wasn't mean, exactly. Just constant. A stream of reminders that I wasn't fluent in the language of belonging. I nodded. I laughed. I swallowed it all. Then I stopped sitting there.

I went back to the white tables. Not because they were better, but because they didn't question me.

They didn't really see me, but they didn't inspect me either.

There's a kind of safety in being misunderstood. At least no one's trying to make you prove anything.

I didn't hate the Black kids. I envied them. Their ease. Their reference points. The way they moved with a kind of cultural memory I didn't have. I was trying to join a family I wasn't raised in, and they smelled the suburb on me.

Every time I opened my mouth, I gave myself away.

They'd tease me about how I dressed. How I talked. What I brought for lunch. The way I held myself like I was bracing for impact. Like I expected to be corrected.

And the truth was: I did.

I felt like I had to earn my Blackness, but didn't know what currency to use.

I started shrinking. Not physically, but inside. I questioned everything. Every laugh. Every sentence. Every song on my playlist. I wondered what part of me was mine, and what part was just mimicry.

And underneath all of it? Shame.

Shame for not knowing the codes. Shame for not growing up with the culture. Shame for being raised by a white woman who thought not seeing race was a form of love.

I used to think proximity to whiteness was protection. But all it really gave me was distance.

I was too "white" for the Black kids. And too Black to ever be anything else to the white ones.

I lived in the space between tables. And no one saved me a seat.

After high school, I thought it might get better. New job. New town. Clean slate.

I started working retail, early twenties, folding shirts under fluorescent lights, pretending not to mind the hours. That's where I met a group of Black coworkers who, for a moment, felt like a doorway. Loud, funny, quick with a roast. They moved through the store like they owned it, even when management didn't.

At first, I stayed quiet. Watched. Took notes. Then I started to ease in.

I'd laugh along, drop a line, mimic the rhythm. One of them said, "Yo, Smith got jokes," and for a second, I felt seen. Like maybe this was it, a place to settle in and belong.

Until one of their friends came in. He was lean, sharp-eyed, a little older. Watched me with the kind of curiosity that wasn't friendly. We were talking about music, I think. Someone brought up Nas. I said something about lyrics, too careful, too formal, and the guy cut me off mid-sentence.

"You sound like a white boy."

It was a joke. Everyone laughed. I laughed too. But it landed like a punch to the ribs.

After he left, I stayed quiet again. The laughter still echoing in my head, hollow and hard. The joke wasn't just about how I spoke, it was about what I wasn't.

I didn't know the references. The music. The slang. The weight behind the words. Every interaction became a test I hadn't studied for, and I was failing it in real time.

I tried harder. Asked questions. Googled slang I didn't understand. I didn't want to fake it, I wanted to earn it. But there was no manual. No syllabus. Just more moments like that one. More side glances. More subtle exclusion wrapped in laughter.

At another job, years later, a Black colleague introduced me to his cousin. We shook hands, brief, casual, and the cousin looked me up and down.

"You Black?"

It wasn't said with hostility. Just disbelief.

"I'm mixed," I answered.

He nodded like he'd already decided.

The conversation moved on, but I didn't.

I never forgot that line. You Black?

Two words that were less a question than a verdict waiting to be confirmed.

I kept working. Kept adjusting. Built a professional mask: calm, articulate, deferential. Around white people, I was the safe one. Around Black people, I was the maybe. The question mark.

And I lived in that limbo, fluent in multiple dialects, fluent in none.

Because the thing no one tells you about being in-between is this:

Every space expects you to translate.

And no one speaks your native tongue.

Too white for the Black kids. Too Black for the white ones.

That line lived in my head like a gospel I never chose to believe in, but couldn't stop repeating.

It wasn't just about who I fit in with. It was about who saw me as real. As whole.

And no one did.

White people saw my skin before my voice. Their praise was always backhanded, "You're so well-spoken," like I should've been slurring or shouting. "You're not like the others," like that was supposed to be a compliment.

Black people saw my posture, my speech, my white upbringing, and called it soft. Or worse, fake.

I didn't have a space. I had spaces I performed in. Adjusted for. Rehearsed around.

I learned early to code-switch before I had a name for it. Shifted how I talked depending on who was in the room. Changed my humor. My cadence. My posture. Like a shapeshifter with a resume. Blend in. Be polite. Don't raise your voice. Don't challenge too hard. Don't confirm their fear of you. Don't confirm their rejection of you.

I thought it was temporary. A phase. But it calcified. Became habit. Then instinct.

I couldn't tell where the mask ended and I began.

And that's the problem with trying to belong to everyone: you end up belonging to no one. Not even yourself.

I started calling it "the box."

Not a literal one. Just... a box of expectation. A set of limits I didn't write, but had to live in.

Too smart? White.

Too angry? Threat.

Too quiet? White again.

Too loud? Problem.

It didn't matter what I felt. It mattered what I looked like.

And once the world sees you a certain way, it's almost impossible to show them anything else.

There's no door out of that box. Just corners. Just walls. Just the echo of your own voice asking, over and over again: "What am I missing?"

That question haunted me.

I didn't want to pick a side. I didn't want to choose whiteness or Blackness like they were teams in gym class. I wanted to be both. Or neither. Or just... me.

But the world doesn't reward nuance. It rewards legibility.

And I was unreadable.

So I adapted.

I wore the clothes that would disarm. Told the jokes that made them laugh. Flattened the parts of me that didn't translate. Built myself into something they could understand, even if I couldn't.

The masks stopped being masks. They became armor. I wasn't performing anymore.

I was surviving.

The first time I worked a job with a lot of Black people, I was told, flat out, that I wasn't really Black.

No metaphor. No implication. Just words, plain and sharp.

"You're not Black for real."

I wasn't called out. I was cut out, excluded from the rhythm, the inside jokes, the cultural shorthand. They didn't trust me. And I got it.

I just endured it.

It wasn't the first time I'd been made to feel like an outsider. But it was the first time it came from people I expected to feel safe with. People who looked like me, at least, enough like me. That's what stung. That's what stuck.

They didn't see me as white. They didn't see me as Black either. They saw me as something in between.

And something in between ain't shit when the world is built on sides.

My skin isn't light enough to pass. Not in the true sense. But it's lighter. Enough to change the equation. Add to that how I speak, how I carry myself, and suddenly, I'm considered safe.

To white people, I'm the good one. Polite. Professional. To Black folks, I'm suspect. Too polished. Too white-adjacent.

Too comfortable in places they had to claw their way into, or were never allowed inside.

I don't blame them.

My white family, they didn't teach me anything about Blackness. How could they?

They were from the far North, near Canada. There are no Black people there. None.

But they didn't try either.

They didn't say the word. Not once. Black was not a race in our house, it was a silence. A permanent erasure.

My father was gone. By the time I understood what "Black" even meant, he was already fading into myth. I did my research later. Dug into the history. Counted the siblings I'll never meet. Traced his bloodline back to Ghana, to Mali.

But the man himself? Gone. He never knew about me.

And I never felt the need to change that.

People ask if I feel guilt, for not struggling the way other Black folks have. For having access. For "sounding white." For fitting in.

I don't.

I was born into what I was born into. I'm not lucky.

I'm just different.

And different is its own kind of weight.

I can't sit in traditional Black spaces and feel at home.

I was raised white. That's my truth. Internally, that's who I identify with. Judge that if you want. I'm done lying about it. I've spent my whole life downplaying both sides.

Not to manipulate. Just to survive.

If I lean too white, I'm a traitor.

If I lean too Black, I'm a threat.

So I live in the crease, always folding, never belonging. All the time.

There's no ease in that.

No privilege. No clarity.

Just performance. Exhaustion. Distance.

But if a kid who looks like me asked, "What am I?"

I'd say: Figure it out now. Quietly. Just for yourself. Because the world will come for you soon enough. And when they try to name you, you say it first.

Say it louder. Say it better. Say it like you mean it. Because you don't owe them an explanation.

Only a warning.

And when I look in the mirror? I see a Black man. Whatever the world thinks that means, that's their confusion.

Not mine.

Chapter Six

The Box

First you learn how to behave to seem proper. Then you learn how to behave so people like you. If you're Black, you also learn how to behave so you seem safe. So you don't get targeted. So you survive.

I don't remember the first time I changed my voice.

But I remember the first time someone noticed.

It was at church. I was maybe twelve. Talking to one of the older women during coffee hour, answering questions the way I'd learned to, in full sentences, with careful grammar, and just enough eye contact to be polite but not challenge. She smiled and said, "You're such a respectful young man."

Then later, outside, with kids my age, different tone, different posture, more slang, shorter sentences. One of them looked at me sideways. "Why you sound different when you talk to grownups?"

I shrugged. Laughed it off. Said I didn't.

But I did. I knew I did.

It was instinct by then, this flicker of awareness that who I was had to shift depending on who was watching. Different rooms, different masks. None of it malicious. Just survival.

Around white people, I softened. Smiled more. Spoke like a thesis paper. Held my hands where they could see them. Never interrupted. Never corrected. Never gave them a reason to flinch.

Around Black folks, I muted the edges of my voice, not because I thought it was wrong, but because I didn't want to sound like I thought I was better. I dropped my pitch, loosened my shoulders, let the rhythm shift.

It wasn't fake. It was fluent.

But fluency isn't the same as comfort.

These weren't choices. They were responses. Trained behaviors. Internal calibrations. I didn't wake up one day and decide to switch, I just learned what kept me safe. What got me liked. What made me understood.

And eventually, I started doing it with everything.

How I dressed. What I laughed at. What I admitted to liking. I learned when to nod, when to hold back, when to say "I know what you mean" even when I didn't. Especially when I didn't.

Some people called it being adaptable.

But I knew better.

It was being fragmented.

And the more I did it, the more the fragments multiplied.

At school, I was the smart one. The polite one. The nonthreatening one. Teachers loved me. I knew how to walk the line, good enough to get praise, not bold enough to make them nervous.

At home, I was quiet. My mom didn't like confrontation. My grandmother liked it even less. There was no room for attitude or pushback. You kept your voice down. You handled your own emotions. You didn't stir the water.

By the time I hit my twenties, I was fluent in about six different versions of myself. Each one tailored. Each one specific.

And every time I switched, I left a piece of myself behind.

That's how it starts, not with a costume, but with a compromise. Small at first. Harmless. Then necessary.

Then permanent.

I was always great on the phone.

That's not ego. Just fact.

I knew how to speak their language: professional, articulate, warm without being too familiar. I asked smart questions. Laughed in the right places. Made them feel comfortable. Safe. Like I was already part of the team.

More than once, I'd hang up knowing the job was mine.

Then I'd show up in person.

And something shifted.

It was subtle, usually. A pause at reception. A flicker in the eyes when they realized I was the same Michael they'd just spoken to. The handshake would tighten, the smile falter for a split second too long.

And I'd feel it.

That quiet recalibration.

They thought I was white.

Not explicitly. Not out loud. But you could hear it in the way they spoke to me on the phone. You could feel it in the ease, the assumption of sameness. And when I walked in, the sameness broke.

They didn't expect me to look like this.

My resume said qualified.

My voice said professional.

My face said something they didn't plan for.

They'd still do the interview. Still smile, still nod, still go through the motions.

But I knew the game. I'd see the shift in real time. The casual tone would stiffen. The questions would turn clinical. They'd glance at my resume like it had betrayed them. Like it had left out something important.

Afterward, I'd get the email: "We've decided to move forward with other candidates."

And sometimes, just to be sure I wasn't imagining it, I'd have a white friend with less experience apply for the same job. He'd get a callback. Sometimes a second interview. Once, he even got the offer.

That's when I stopped assuming my qualifications were enough.

I started tailoring everything. Not just the resume, but the whole performance.

Polished shoes. Neutral tie. Clean haircut. Firm handshake. Open body language. Never too assertive. Never too casual. Just the right amount of confidence to be impressive, but not intimidating.

The goal was simple: don't scare them.

I wasn't just applying for a job. I was auditioning for acceptability. Because the risk wasn't that they'd hate me. It was that they'd be uncomfortable.

And discomfort, in corporate America, is the kiss of death. You don't need to be the best. You just need to feel familiar. So I became a master of familiarity.

Smiled without showing too much teeth. Paused before answering questions. Dropped in cultural references they'd recognize. Spoke like a TED Talk with good posture.

It worked.

Eventually, they stopped seeing me as Black. They saw me as "professional."
Which, in that world, meant the same thing.

It was supposed to be a regular afternoon.

My son and I were driving through one of those wealthy white towns where the sidewalks are wide, the mailboxes are designer, and the police drive slow, not to protect, just to observe.

We were at a red light when a car behind us didn't stop in time. Teenage girl. Distracted. Her dad's SUV. Fender tap, nothing serious. I checked on my son, then stepped out to look at the damage.

She was already crying.

The cop showed up fast. Two of them. One stayed by her, comforting, clipboard out. The other came to me.

Not friendly. Not hostile. Just alert.

I explained what happened. Calm. Precise. My voice in that practiced register, low enough to sound in control, clear enough to be non-threatening. I kept my hands visible. Smiled more than I needed to. Gave them no excuse.

Still, the questions came like bullets with silencers.

"Where were you coming from?"

"Is this your car?"

"Do you have ID on you?"

"Is the child yours?"

The girl admitted fault. The story didn't change. But the scrutiny stayed on me. Like they were waiting for me to twitch.

Eventually, there was nothing left to poke.

The cop's tone shifted, just a little.

He handed me back my license, stepped back, and said, "You're one of the good ones."

Just like that. Like I should be grateful.

I nodded. Said nothing.

Got in the car. Closed the door.

My son asked, "What did he mean?"

I told him it didn't matter. But it did. It mattered more than the accident. More than the paperwork. More than whether the bumper would need replacing.

Because that line, "You're one of the good ones," is never neutral.

It's a pat on the head with a collar underneath.

It says: You are acceptable to me because you didn't make me uncomfortable. Because you didn't raise your voice. Because you played your part.

Because you behaved.

It's not a compliment. It's a reminder. That your safety is conditional. That your worth is measured by how little you make them squirm. That your dignity is a currency you're expected to spend just to survive the day.

I drove us home in silence.

Didn't turn on the radio. Didn't call anyone. Didn't tell my wife until later. It wasn't new. It wasn't shocking. It was just... exhausting.

That's the part people don't understand. It's not the moment itself. It's the accumulation. The thousand quiet slaps you swallow. The rage you repurpose into silence. The way you teach your own child how to disappear in plain sight, for his own protection.

I wasn't angry.

I was tired.

Tired of proving I'm safe.

Chapter Seven

The Good One

It started early.

Third grade, maybe. Maybe earlier. Someone tossed me a dodgeball and said, "Bet you're fast." I was. But the way they said it, like a prophecy, not a compliment, landed wrong. Like they already knew who I was before I did.

That's how it always went.

Strong. Fast. Athletic.

Not smart.

No one ever said I was dumb. Not directly. But the praise always bent toward surprise. "Wow, you're really good at math." "You read a lot, huh?" "You're so articulate."

Articulate.

Four syllables that mean: "I didn't expect this from someone like you."

At first, I took it as a win. I thought I was standing out. Thought it meant I was doing something right.

Then I realized: I was being measured against a deficit they never named.

They didn't expect me to be smart. They didn't expect me to be gentle. They didn't expect me to be anything but physical, and maybe funny, if I smiled enough.

I was strong. That made sense to them.

I was fast. That made them feel correct.

But when I asked questions? When I corrected a teacher? When I offered an answer that wasn't surface-level?

Something tightened in the room.

And I learned to watch for that. Learned to ease off the gas when I was too far ahead. Learned to give just enough, never too much. Never more than they were ready to receive from someone who looked like me.

Because the moment I stepped out of the box, I was either suspicious, or exceptional.

And both are prisons.

One kid at school, white, hockey player, always carried a Monster Energy drink, once said, "You're like, not even Black. You're just Mike."

He meant it as acceptance. Meant it as praise.

What I heard was: your identity doesn't matter as long as I don't have to deal with it.

That's what being "the good one" means.

It means shrinking the parts of yourself that make others uncomfortable. Performing safety. Predictability. Humor, when needed. Strength, when called for. Silence, when expected.

It means becoming a version of Black that fits their narrative.

Strong, but never aggressive.

Smart, but never condescending.

Proud, but never political.

I became fluent in that performance. Mastered it. Aced interviews. Navigated white spaces like I'd built them myself. People loved me. Admired me.

But only because they'd mistaken me for something I wasn't.

Safe.

And every time they told me how good I was, how respectful, how well-spoken, how impressive, I smiled. I nodded.

And underneath, something curled into a fist.

Because I knew what they meant.

They meant: "Thank you for not making us deal with who you really are."

They didn't catch me stealing.

They just assumed I had.

It was middle school. Convenience store. I had a dollar in my pocket and a pack of gum in my hand. The clerk, tall, red-faced, beard like steel wool, never took his eyes off me. Not once.

I paid for the gum. Took my change. Walked out.

Next time I came in, he followed me. Just close enough to make sure I knew.

"Looking for anything in particular?"

"No, just Browse."

"Well, let me know if you need help."

I didn't. But he kept asking. Every aisle. Every corner.

The message was clear: I wasn't there to buy. I was there to be watched.

That was the beginning. After that, it became routine.

Teachers assuming I was the one talking during quiet work time.

Substitute accusing me of cheating on a quiz, even though I was the only one who had studied.

Security guard stopping me at the mall.

Librarian asking if I had a card, even though I came in every week.

It wasn't rage, at first. It was confusion. Embarrassment. That hollow shame that follows you home and crawls into bed with you.

I started double-checking my pockets before I left stores. Made sure tags were visible. Kept my hands out in the open. Smiled more.

Not because I was afraid of getting caught, but because I was tired of being suspected.

Then one day, I did it.

I stole something.

Nothing big, a CD from Walmart. Slipped it into my coat. Walked out calm. No one stopped me.

It wasn't about needing it. It was about control. About flipping the narrative. Proving, in a twisted way, that if they were going to treat me like a thief, I might as well take something.

They built the box first. Then dared me to fit inside it. And when I did, even just once, it felt like confirmation.

To them. To me.

After that, I went back to performing. Back to polite. Back to clean and careful and responsible. But a crack had opened.

Because deep down, I knew the truth:

They didn't see me as innocent until proven guilty.

They saw me as guilty until proven acceptable.

And even then, just barely.

Sometimes I was followed in stores. Sometimes I wasn't.

But even when I wasn't, I felt like I was. That's the thing. You don't need eyes on you to act like they're there. Once it happens a few times, it becomes muscle memory.

Walk in. Nod at the cashier. Keep your hands visible. Don't linger. Don't loiter. Don't touch anything you're not buying. Move like you belong, but not like you're too comfortable.

Keep your hood down. Keep your bag zipped. Keep your face neutral.

Smile, but not too much.

It's not fear. It's choreography.

I call it "the Black autopilot." The quiet recalibration that happens every time I enter a space where I'm the only one. Especially white neighborhoods. Upscale shops. Offices. Parks at dusk. Places where presence alone feels like a provocation.

There was one night, I was walking back to my car from a friend's house. Cold, quiet street. A white woman was ahead of me on the sidewalk. She looked back. Then again.

I crossed the street.

Not because I was doing anything wrong, but because I didn't want her fear to become my problem.

I've done that more times than I can count.

Changed my path. Slowed my pace. Coughed or shuffled to make my presence known in the least threatening way possible.

Because I'm not allowed to be invisible.

But I'm not allowed to be seen, either.

Same thing in the car. If I get pulled over, I narrate everything out loud. Hands on the wheel. Window halfway down. License already out. "Yes, officer." "No, sir." "Just going home."

I make sure my tone is calm. Not annoyed. Not defiant. Calm.

Even when I've done nothing wrong. Especially when I've done nothing wrong.

Because the wrong reaction to the wrong assumption can turn into a headline.

That's the part that never gets explained properly. It's not that we expect to be shot. It's that we expect not to be believed. So we overcompensate.

We train ourselves to look harmless. Sound harmless. Be harmless. Even when we're angry. Even when we're afraid. Even when we're right.

Because being right won't keep you safe. Not in a system built to see you as a threat before you say a word.

This isn't about paranoia.

It's about practice.

A lifetime of practice.

And me? I got "lucky."

I was raised in a white town. Got a white education. Made white connections. Because I was the only one, I got treated like a charity case.

People made room. Gave me chances. Gave me help.

So I learned what they learned. Read what they read. Spoke how they spoke. And that gave me an edge, at least at first.

Then I hit the real world. In phone interviews, I was perfect. Polished. Hireable. But when I showed up in person?

Some faces fell.

They were expecting white.
They got me.

Others saw me as a safe bet, a two-fer. Hire me, and they could check the box without changing the culture.

I was their token Black guy.

I knew it. They knew it. We all played along.

But once I was in the building? I had to work three times as hard as less-qualified white colleagues just to be seen.

And if I got tired? If I stopped pushing? They whispered it anyway: "See? Told you."

You carry the weight of a whole race on your shoulders, and if you stumble once, they call it proof.

And still, I was lucky. Because I even got hired.

In one job, I noticed something. I posted job openings. HR reviewed applicants, and somehow, every "qualified" candidate they gave me to review was white.

So I did something simple: I told HR I'd screen the resumes myself. And just like that, Black candidates appeared.

Not a flood. But enough to prove the lie: they were always there.

Just filtered out before they had a chance.

And even though I know how the game is played, even though I've seen behind the curtain, there's only so much I can do. Not alone. Not against a system that was never broken.

Just built this way.

I'm not blind. Just tired. I'm tired of proving I'm safe.

Tired of adjusting my tone so I don't sound angry.

Tired of softening my face so I don't look aggressive.

Tired of explaining who I am before I'm allowed to be it.

I'm tired of calculating. Every conversation. Every entrance. Every gesture.

Tired of decoding what they mean when they say "You're not like the others."

Tired of being their favorite example. Their exception. Their buffer.

Tired of having to be better just to be considered equal.

Tired of being "one of the good ones."

Tired of pretending that "articulate" is a compliment.

Tired of hearing "we're so glad you're here" and knowing what that really means.

I've spent a lifetime performing safety.

And no matter how perfectly I play the role, I'm still treated like the story they wrote before I walked in.

A risk. A box. A shadow.

I used to think if I just worked harder, if I stayed polite, stayed sharp, stayed calm, they'd see me.

Now I know better.

They don't want to see me.

They want to feel good about not seeing what I am.

And I'm done.

Done shrinking.

Done code-switching out of survival.

Done letting their comfort define my character.

I'm not here to be manageable.

I'm here.

Full stop.

Chapter Eight

The Masks I Wore

I knew I had the job before I walked in.

The phone screen had gone perfectly. I'd hit all the notes: confident, articulate, just the right edge of humor. I could hear the warmth in the recruiter's voice. She called me "impressive." Said I had "executive presence."

Then I showed up.

The woman at the front desk did a double take when I said my name.

A man came out to greet me. His smile was just a second too late. Eyes scanning. Recalculating.

We shook hands. His grip was firm. So was his shift in tone.

He asked the same questions we'd already covered. This time, with a different rhythm. More formal. More guarded. I answered anyway: polished, precise, perfect.

Because I knew the mask he wanted.

Professional. Polite. Nonthreatening. The safe Black guy with a tech brain and a good handshake.

I gave him everything he came for.

He smiled at the end, said, "You're a great fit."

But the smile didn't reach his eyes.

And I left the building with a familiar taste in my mouth: something like metal, something like bitterness.

He saw the version of me I'd spent years refining. And he still couldn't picture me in the seat.

Because I wasn't just interviewing for a job.

I was auditioning for acceptability.

Again.

Sometimes, late at night, I stand in the bathroom and stare at the mirror.

Not out of vanity, but out of curiosity.

I look at my face and try to name which version of me is staring back.

The Work Mask? The one that smiles on cue, folds its hands, listens just enough, never interrupts, speaks in phrases like "data-driven approach" and "strategic alignment"?

The White Room Mask? That voice I slide into when I walk into a meeting full of executives, or a coffee shop full of stares. Clear. Cordial. Friendly. Just enough to say I belong. Not enough to say I'm a threat.

The Black Room Mask? That careful relaxation. Looser shoulders. Different cadence. A nod instead of a handshake. Casual familiarity I've practiced more than I've lived.

The Interview Mask.

The Networking Mask.

The In-Law Mask.

The Parent-Teacher Conference Mask.

The masks aren't lies.

They're defenses.

They're translations.

They're the cost of moving through a world that demands I explain myself before I'm allowed to be myself.

I've worn every kind of mask.

The smart one.

The humble one.

The overachiever.

The safe Black guy.

The one who doesn't get offended.

The one who takes the joke.

The one who laughs with you before he burns.

The one who doesn't bring up race.

The one who does, but gently.

They all work, if you commit.

If you wear them long enough, they harden. They hold. They get you the job, the nod, the safety.

But they come with a cost.

And that cost is this: after a while, you forget what your face looks like without them.

You forget what your voice sounds like when it's not adjusting for someone else.

I look in the mirror and try to find the version of me that isn't performing.

And most nights?

I don't see him.

I told her one night. Not all of it. Just enough to crack the shell.

We were lying in bed. Lights off. That time of night when everything's quieter and truer. I was staring at the ceiling, still wired from the day. She was next to me, reading. Something small. Fiction.

I said, "I'm tired."

She looked over. "Yeah?"

"Not work tired," I added. "Not body tired. Just... tired of performing."

That got her attention.

I sat up a little, arms around my knees. Couldn't quite look at her. Just spoke into the dark like it might absorb the parts I couldn't hold.

"I don't know who I am without the performance. Every room I walk into, I have to become someone else. At work, I'm articulate and agreeable. Around Black folks, I try not to sound like I grew up in the woods. Around white folks, I soften my tone, make sure I don't sound angry."

A pause.

"I don't even know what my real voice sounds like anymore."

She didn't say anything right away.

Didn't reach to fix it. Didn't try to reframe it. Just listened.

That's what I needed.

Not advice. Not optimism.

Just someone to witness it.

To sit in the heaviness with me without trying to sweep it up.

Finally, she said, "I can't imagine what that's like."

I nodded. "Yeah."

"But I want to understand it better. I want to hear it, when you're ready."

That mattered more than I had words for.

Because most people, even the good ones, don't know how to hold space for that kind of exhaustion.

They want solutions. Action steps. A next move.

But some things don't need to be solved.

They need to be seen.

That night, I didn't unmask. Not fully. But something cracked. A seam opened.

And for the first time in a long time, I felt a little less alone inside my own performance.

Chapter Nine

Merit-Based

The system works. Just not for everyone.

Actually, that's not true.

The system works exactly the way it was designed:

To keep people right where they are.

I've heard people say, "The system's broken."

It's not.

It's functioning exactly the way it was built.

I've lived it.

I've worked twice as hard for half the visibility. I've trained white interns who got promoted before I did. I've sat in meetings where I had to prove I wasn't just "passionate," but precise.

This isn't a theory for me. It's my Tuesday.

Black people are kept in their modern-day reservations, the inner city.

Our political power is stripped through gerrymandering. Our schools are underfunded. That leads to lower test scores. Lower graduation rates. Lower-paying jobs. Fewer qualifications. Less economic mobility. Fewer home loans.

And just like that, we're back where we started. Still on "The Rez". Still boxed in.

This is not hypothetical. This is fact.

We are pulled over more. Arrested more. Locked up more.

And now, instead of fixing any of it, the response is to kill "wokeness." Abolish DEI. Reverse Affirmative Action.

All in the name of "merit."

Sounds noble, on paper. Until you realize the playing field has never been level. And was never meant to be.

If you underfund Black schools, deny Black students equal access, and then say we all have to compete "on merit,"

What merit are we measuring?

We can't win a rigged game. And they know it. They like it that way.

This isn't a glitch. It's the blueprint.

One job saw "potential" in me. They assigned me mentors. Said they believed in me. What they meant was: I was safe enough to polish and put in front of white executives without setting off alarms.

So who did they assign me?

The only other mixed leader in the company.

I could see why. He played the part well. Sharp. Polished. Never talked about race. Definitely didn't sound like he was from the country.

He tried to give me advice: how to move, how to play the game. I kept trying to break the script. Pushed him. Raised race. Asked hard questions.

He never took the bait. I could see it in his eyes, he wanted to say something real. But he didn't.

Six meetings. Nothing.

Until he moved.

Left Fairbridge. Took his wife and kids south. Said it was for opportunity. Better house. Better schools.

A year later, I reached out. Didn't expect much. But this time?

He spoke.

Told me he feared for his family. Told me the racism was louder than expected. Said they were coming back.

And for once, I was proud of him. Not for surviving, but for finally saying it out loud.

But it didn't last.

He moved back. Slid right back into the role. No more hard truths. Just strategy, posture, polish.

And I get it. It's safer that way. But now I know he saw it too.

When the mentorship failed, they nominated me for something else: a year-long executive development program.

I was ecstatic.

I thought they finally saw me. Thought I was being fast-tracked. That I'd earned something.

Then I found out, it was a program for Black leaders.

And just like that, the pride twisted in my chest.

Fuck me.

I still took it. It was a good opportunity. But it hurt in ways I wasn't prepared for.

There were thirty of us. And only two mixed folks.

There was a team-building session early on.

They passed around a mic. Each person had to say where they were from, what high school they went to, and one moment that made them proud to be Black.

My throat dried out instantly.

The guy before me talked about marching with his dad. The woman after him talked about her HBCU homecoming.

When it got to me, I froze. I said something vague about "resilience."

Nobody said anything, but I felt the shift.

Later, one of the participants pulled me aside. Said, "You're cool, but… you different."

I nodded like I didn't already know.

Like I hadn't heard that my whole life.

Different wasn't neutral. Different meant not from here. Different meant not family.

I watched the other mixed guy keep his mask on, tight. Trying to blend. Trying to prove his Blackness without overdoing it. I knew that game. I'd played it too long.

But in that room? I couldn't hold it.

Everyone else spoke like family. Like they'd lived the same storm. I hadn't. And they knew it. They could smell it. See it in my eyes. My mask cracked under the weight of too many eyes. Too much knowing.

I talked to my program mentor. Told him I felt out of place. He said I was imagining things.

We both knew better.

I made it through. Completed the program. Four years later, the group chat's still active.

I read it sometimes. I never type. Not because I'm angry, but because I still don't feel like I belong.

And yet, when I list it on my résumé, it sounds like a badge:

Leadership initiative. Executive track. Merit-based.

But I know what got me in. And I know why I still feel like a stranger.

The game isn't about talent. It's about presentation. It's about proximity to comfort. And comfort has never looked like me.

In a perfect world, everything could be merit-based. And honestly, in theory? It still makes sense. But the gap between people is too wide for that logic to hold. The disparity is baked in. The race starts uneven.

And now? People like me don't just have to work four times harder on the job, we have to work four times harder just to get the job.

There's no such thing as a blind resume. Once they know who you are, what you are, the bar moves. The bar always moves.

So yeah. Merit-based makes sense. But only in a world where everything is equal.

We don't live in that world. Not today. Not in the foreseeable future.

Chapter Ten

Stuck

The first time I realized I was wearing a mask, I was eight.

It didn't look like a mask. It looked like "manners."

It sounded like, "You're so well-behaved."

It felt like approval. Like safety. Like passing.

I learned to nod. To smile.

To be agreeable.

To tone it down when I was angry.

To laugh off the jokes.

To sit with discomfort and call it patience.

At first, it wasn't even conscious.

It was survival.

I was the only Black kid in school, in church, on the block.

There was no one to tell me what to hold onto, so I clung to whatever kept me from standing out.

The mask worked.

Teachers loved me.

Parents trusted me.

Cops didn't flinch when they saw me.

I learned how to be safe.

But I also learned something else:

If you wear a mask long enough, people stop looking for what's underneath.

And worse?

So do you.

There's a point where adaptation becomes erasure.

Where fitting in becomes fading out.

I told myself I wasn't like other Black kids, not because I believed I was better, but because I thought that was the only way I'd be accepted.

Not just by white people.

By anyone.

Because when I did try to belong in Black spaces, I was called out for sounding white. For not knowing the references. For not being "down."

So I drifted.

Too white for the Black kids.

Too Black for the white ones.

Too mixed to be either.

Too coded to be free.

I stopped asking where I belonged.

I just tried to blend.

I became fluent in whiteness.

Not just language, but posture. Performance. Timing.

Knowing when to speak and when to shut up.

When to joke and when to disappear.

People call that emotional intelligence.

I call it exhaustion.

The worst part wasn't the pretending.

It was that I got good at it.

Promoted for it.

Rewarded for it.

The mask didn't just protect me.

It advanced me.

And somewhere along the way, I stopped knowing where it ended and I began.

That's what nobody tells you about code-switching:

If you're not careful, the switch becomes default.

I wasn't lying.

I was editing.

Every room, a different draft of me.

Every interaction, a new line cut for clarity.

Until one day, I couldn't remember what the original sounded like.

And that's the danger.

Not that the world forces you to wear a mask.

But that you start believing it fits.

Wearing masks has become a staple of what I do. Not in the Halloween sense. Not in the COVID sense. In the how do I survive this meeting without becoming a stereotype sense. In the how do I walk into this white room and walk back out with my dignity, my sanity, and my paycheck sense.

Some of them are tactical. Necessary. Protection as strategy. A different face for each environment. A version of me that can't be used as a weapon.

But there's one mask I wore so long, it fused.

The one that makes my race more palatable. The one that eases the tension in the room. The one that makes white people feel like they know me.

That mask got stuck.

It fit so tightly, and for so long, it became second skin. I started to forget I was wearing it. That it wasn't actually me. That I didn't come into the world smiling for their comfort.

I think the first time I put it on, I was twelve. A teacher told my mother I was "so well-spoken." She said it with a smile like she'd just unwrapped a gift. I didn't know what it meant back then. But I remember how proud my mom looked. And I remember how small I felt. Like I had done something right by being less threatening.

By the time I got my first job, I already knew the drill. You don't speak first. You don't correct people. You don't flinch when the joke stings. You let them believe they're progressive just for being near you. And if you're lucky, they'll call you "one of the good ones."

I laughed off semi-racist jokes from peers. I swallowed the sharp breath when someone made a comment they thought was clever. I stayed quiet when someone asked me to speak for my entire race, as if I was the designated spokesperson for Black America.

I heard about another police shooting in Lakemont, another car stop turned coffin, and had to act like I was fine with it. Because I had a work trip there. Because I had to present in a conference room full of people who would rather talk about bandwidth than brutality.

George Floyd was murdered and I had to pretend it was just another Tuesday. Smile. Numb. Keep it moving.

I listened to people say we needed "a certain number of minorities" in the candidate pool for VP-level positions, but only for appearances. Heard them say it out loud, in rooms with coffee and catered pastries, like it was logistics, not lives.

I read monthly reports that track how many minorities and women are in our division. As if I'm not one of them. As if I'm not the reason those numbers exist.

And when I asked for that same data? I was told it was sensitive.

That's the gaslight. They want you visible, but not too informed.

Do you know what it feels like to sit in a group of 200 technologists and know you're one of fewer than ten Black people? And to realize you hired four of them yourself?

Is that a coincidence?

Or is it that I evaluated skillsets honestly, and just didn't filter out the names that made other hiring managers flinch?

How many times do I have to act grateful when someone says, "Happy MLK Day!" like it's a damn party? Or when they wish me a "Happy Juneteenth" like they're handing me a cupcake instead of commemorating a delay in freedom?

I swear to God, it's enough to drive someone insane.

The fact that I don't lose my shit in those moments should qualify me for an Oscar. The restraint. The poise. The forced "Thanks" I deliver with a smile tight enough to crack a tooth.

And you know what I really want to say?

Don't wish me Happy Juneteenth unless you're ready to talk about reparations. Don't wish me a Happy MLK Day unless you understand that man was murdered by the same comfort you're hiding behind now. Don't thank me for being professional when what you mean is, "Thanks for making us feel better about doing nothing."

I've clenched my jaw so hard in meetings that I've left with headaches. I've smiled through so many comments I stopped noticing when my neck tightened. I've mastered silence so completely that sometimes I forget what my actual voice sounds like.

I've spent entire days performing so well that by the time I got home, I couldn't find the real me underneath. I'd sit in silence for hours, just trying to remember how to speak without adjusting every syllable for someone else's comfort.

And the worst part? They never notice. They just nod and move on.

Because that's what the mask is for.

That's what it does.

It keeps them comfortable. It keeps me contained.

And I've worn it so well, so convincingly, for so long…

they think it's my face.

I used to think this mask was protection. But lately, it feels like a muzzle. And I'm ready to tear it off.

Chapter Eleven

Filling Out Forms

It was the last page of the packet, the checkbox.

Race: (Select one)

☐ White

☐ African American

☐ Asian

☐ Hispanic/Latino

☐ Pacific Islander

☐ Native American

☐ Other

Pick one.

As if the rest of me didn't exist. As if blood could be categorized into neat ink boxes. As if the hardest thing about being mixed was deciding where to file the paperwork.

I sat there with the pen in my hand, hovering.

Technically, I'm both. Half. Whole. Neither.

But that wasn't an option.

Some forms let you check more than one. Some give you "Two or more races." Some offer "Other," like you're a glitch in the system. A data point they haven't figured out how to graph yet.

But this one?

This one wanted clarity.

Which, for me, has always been code for conformity.

I used to check "White," just to fuck with them. Just to see if the follow-up call had a different tone.

Other times I'd check "Black," because that's what the world sees. That's what the cop sees when he pulls me over. That's what the recruiter sees when I walk in. That's what the neighborhood sees when I knock on a door they didn't expect me at.

But every time I do it, I feel like I'm betraying something.

Not because either part of me is wrong, but because neither part is enough.

I thought about just leaving it blank.

But I've done that before. They send the form back. Say it's incomplete. Say they need the data for reporting.

What they need is permission.

They need you to consent to being simplified.

To make their job easier.

To fit into their version of you, the one that's easier to track, easier to explain, easier to ignore when things go wrong.

So I crossed them all out.

And in big, block letters, wrote: MIXED.

No box. Just truth.

Let them figure it out.

Let them try to format that into a report.

Let them squint at the form and ask what category that belongs to. It belongs to me.

The box followed me everywhere.

School enrollment forms.

Standardized tests.

College applications.

Financial aid.

Loan documents.

Job portals.

Medical intake sheets.

Every institution wanted a piece of me boiled down into one word.

Pick one.

It started in elementary school. I remember asking my mom what I should select. She said, "Put Black. That's what people see."

That was the first time I realized the form wasn't about identity, it was about perception. About how the world would sort me before I opened my mouth.

In high school, one of my teachers handed back a state test and said, "You really beat the odds."

I asked what odds.

She pointed at the demographic report stapled to the back.

Black. Male. Rural.

And somehow, still… gifted.

She meant it as praise. What I heard was: "You weren't supposed to do this well."

That's what those boxes do.

They shape the expectations before you even arrive.

Later, in college applications, I started playing the game.

Check Black, maybe it helps me get in.

Check White, maybe I don't raise a red flag.

Check nothing, maybe they'll guess and I can dodge the whole thing.

But they always guess.

And they always default to the part of you that feels like risk.

Job interviews were the worst. I'd crush the phone screen, friendly, polished, sharp. I could feel the energy shift, hear the eagerness in their voice. "We can't wait to meet you in person!"

Then I'd show up. And they'd blink. Smile too long. Recalculate. Ask if I needed help finding the building.

They thought they were hiring the version of me that matched the résumé. The one their mind pictured. The one they assumed. The box didn't just follow me.

It preceded me.

It arrived before I did. Whispered ahead. Shaped the room I walked into. And I adapted.

Every space, every form, every interaction, I got better at becoming what they expected. What made them comfortable. What fit inside the parameters they'd assigned me.

But after a while, I didn't know what I was adjusting from.

I just knew I wasn't being seen. Not fully.

I was being categorized.

Boxed.

And once you've been flattened into data points long enough, you start wondering if anything real about you even registers anymore.

I stopped filling out forms the way they wanted.

Not loudly. Not as a protest. Just... quietly. A refusal.

Whenever I saw that line, Race: Select one, I'd draw a slash through it. Write "Mixed" in the margin. Sometimes in block letters. Sometimes cursive. Sometimes just a single word, scrawled like a dare. I stopped playing the game.

No more checking "Black" to make someone's diversity metrics look better. No more checking "White" to slip past the assumptions. No more "Other" like I was some fringe case they hadn't figured out how to market yet.

I started writing in the truth.

Even when I knew it would cause problems.

Even when I knew it meant someone at a desk would roll their eyes and send the form back.

Even when I knew it knew it meant another delay, another question, another awkward pause.

That was the point. Let them pause. Let them have to read it. Let them squint and say, "Mixed with what?"

Let them sit in the discomfort of not knowing how to label me.

That discomfort? That's mine, every damn day.

So they can hold it for thirty seconds.

It's a small rebellion. A scribble. An inconvenience. But it's also a declaration. That my identity isn't a checkbox. That my life doesn't fit in your clean little categories.

That I'm not going to simplify myself for your sorting system. It's not activism. It's not performance. It's survival. It's clarity.

It's the slow, deliberate work of reclaiming narrative control. One form at a time.

Chapter Twelve

Rage is Not a Crime

They asked me to speak.

Not because I'd volunteered. Not because I had experience. But because I was Black. And visible. And calm enough to put in front of a crowd.

This was after George Floyd. After the statements. After the LinkedIn posts with black squares and hashtags that felt like branding more than mourning. The company sent an email to the division: We believe in unity. In healing. In hard conversations. They called it a listening session.

Then they handed me the mic.

I knew what they wanted.

A measured story. Some vulnerability. Just enough edge to feel authentic, not enough to make them squirm. They wanted affirmation dressed as accountability. But I had other plans.

I made slides. Pulled numbers. Looked at our company's diversity reports: board members, senior leadership, hiring stats. Looked at the national data. Looked at our local data. Built a case. Clear. Undeniable. Black and white, literally.

And then I added one slide at the end. Just one.

It showed the racial composition of our leadership team. All white. All male. All smiling. I saved it for last.

When the day came, I stood in front of the auditorium. Lights in my face. CIO in the front row. Boss beside him. Both watching me like they were hoping for a sermon but bracing for a storm.

I was already nervous giving the speech. Big auditorium. Full of peers. Simulcast to another site and streamed overseas. Cameras everywhere. Recorded. Permanent. Sitting on the corporate intranet for anyone to watch, rewind, dissect. For someone like me, who needed things to go exactly right to survive public scrutiny, it was already too much.

And then, the slide was missing.

I froze. Clicked back. Then forward. Then back again. Maybe I was wrong. Maybe I'd misordered it. But no. It was just gone.

My most direct critique. The visual proof. The numbers. The faces. The thing that tied all of it together, deleted. I looked down at my notes. The line referencing it was still there.

I looked at the front row. The CIO just sat there. Shrugging. And in that instant, I stopped panicking.

I got angry.

This wasn't a glitch. This was a muzzle. So I looked out at the audience and said, "Well, it looks like I'm missing a slide, but I have notes, so let's go on."

And I gave the rest of the speech. From memory. Pointed. Measured. Sharp.

Guess what?

It was never posted to the intranet. Before the presentation, I'd asked HR for a breakdown of minority leadership representation. What the numbers were. How they'd changed over time.

They refused. Said it wasn't authorized.

Translation: They knew.

The next morning, I was called into a meeting. Not with HR. Not with legal. Just my boss, David Langley, and a chair pulled too far from the table.

He smiled when I walked in. That tight, managerial kind of smile, where every tooth feels like a warning.

"Michael," he said, "yesterday's session was... intense."

I nodded. Sat. Said nothing.

He tapped a pen on the folder in front of him. No paper inside. Just the gesture. Just the power.

"We appreciate your passion. Really. But some of your comments caught people off guard. It didn't feel... constructive."

There it was. *Constructive.*

That word they use when you've stopped asking for permission. When you've stopped making them feel safe in their own mess.

I didn't apologize.

He kept going. "We'd like to reframe the conversation a bit. Shift the tone. More focus on progress, less on,"

"Truth?" I said.

He paused. Just for a second.

"I was going to say conflict."

He offered me an out. A chance to rewrite the moment. Reshape the message. Walk it back.

I said no. I quit the D&I role that day.

Told him I'd stay on in my actual job, the one I was hired to do. The one that didn't require me to make the company feel better about itself. He said he understood.

He didn't.

What he understood was that I wasn't going to play the mascot anymore. That I wasn't going to sit in the front row of their guilt parade and wave.

After that, the temperature shifted. Fewer emails. Fewer invites. Less eye contact in the halls. The corporate version of being ghosted.

But at home? Rachel saw it.

Saw how I walked in that night, quiet but charged. Saw the look on my face before I said anything.

"What happened?" she asked. I told her everything.

She didn't say "I'm proud of you."

She didn't say "That was brave."

She said, "Do you want to quit?"

I didn't have an answer.

She nodded. Waited. Let the silence be a safe place. Then she said, "Whatever you decide, I've got you."

That was enough. I didn't need a solution. I needed to know someone still saw me when the masks came off.

A few weeks later, I was invited to a leadership training.

Offsite. Neutral ground. No podiums. No statements. Just managers from across departments, trying to learn how to lead better, or at least, how to perform like they were trying. There was a breakout session about bias. The facilitator, a young white woman with a TED Talk smile, asked everyone to share a "challenge" they'd experienced in the workplace.

People took turns.

"My team struggles with communication."

"I'm learning how to manage up."

"We need more women in tech."

Each statement polished. Professional. Digestible. Then it was my turn.

I could feel the tension before I opened my mouth. I was one of two Black people in the room. The other had stayed silent the whole time. I looked around. Took a breath.

Then I said: "I don't know if I'm getting opportunities because I'm good at what I do, or because I'm Black."

Silence. Not the polite kind. The kind that hits like a slap.

Someone shifted in their chair. Someone else exhaled through their nose, sharp, controlled, like they were bracing for a storm that hadn't come yet.

The facilitator smiled too wide. "Thank you for sharing, Michael. That's very... vulnerable." She moved on.

But the room didn't recover.

Afterward, a few people came up to me. A couple thanked me. One woman touched my arm and said, "I can't imagine." Others avoided eye contact. Walked past like I'd broken some unwritten code. Like I'd pulled something private into the light and made it impossible to look away.

But that was the point.

I didn't share that to inspire empathy. I shared it because it was true.

Because I've spent a lifetime working twice as hard, only to question whether I earned any of it. Because every win carries an asterisk, quiet, implied, heavy.

Because no matter how polished I become, there's always someone wondering if I'm here to check a box. And some days? That someone is me.

Later, a younger employee found me by the coffee station.

She was Black. Maybe early twenties. Nervous. Like she wasn't sure if she was allowed to say what she wanted to say. "I just wanted to thank you," she said. "For saying that. I think about it all the time, but I've never heard anyone say it out loud."

I nodded. Said, "You're not the only one."

And for the first time in weeks, I believed that maybe I wasn't, either.

Chapter Thirteen

I'm Not a Box

I am not your assumption.

I am not your checkbox.

I am not your story to tell.

I am not "African American" because you need it on a spreadsheet. I am not "Other" because you couldn't figure out how to fit me in. I am not your teachable moment.

I am not articulate for a Black man. I am not impressive for someone "like me." I am not lucky to be here.

I'm here because I worked. Because I bled for the seat. Because I learned to speak your language better than you ever bothered to learn mine.

I remember one performance review where I exceeded every metric. Led two cross-functional teams. Saved the company a quarter million. My manager said, "You're a rising star. You're lucky leadership is focused on diversity right now."

Lucky.

That word bruised worse than any punch I've taken. I wasn't lucky. I was exhausted. And still, somehow, expected to smile and say thank you.

That's the game. Break your back and still feel like you have to earn your place every day.

I do not exist to validate your quota. I do not exist to make you feel evolved. I do not exist to ease your guilt or elevate your optics.

I am not here to be tolerated. I am not here to be explained. I am not here to be safe for you.

I'm a person. Not a box.

And if you need a box to know what I am, you're not ready to know me.

You can try to shrink me into one word. But that word will never carry where I'm from, what I've survived, what I carry in the silence.

You want to talk diversity? Then start by letting me be more than your data.

You want inclusion? Then stop asking me to subtract pieces of myself to belong.

You want equity? Then give me the freedom to bring all of me, not just the parts that make you comfortable.

I don't need your approval. I don't need your allyship if it only works in daylight.

I am not here to play a role in your redemption arc.

I'm not your quota. I'm not your mascot. I'm not your test case. I'm not your Black friend.

I'm me.

And I'm done asking for permission to exist in full.

If you've made it this far, then maybe you see it.

The weight.

Not just the stories, but the shape they leave behind. The way they bend your spine even when no one's looking. The way they settle into your lungs until every breath feels filtered through expectation.

This wasn't written to make you comfortable.

I'm not trying to inspire you. Or educate you. Or convert you.

I'm trying to say something out loud that I was never allowed to say in rooms that claimed to care about me.

That being mixed in America isn't a bridge.

It's a fracture.

It's not just a fracture. It's a fault line. And I've spent years building a life on top of it, smiling, succeeding, sounding "safe." Waiting for the day it all cracks open.

I've had white coworkers ask if I was "urban" enough to weigh in on Black issues. Black peers ask if I "even count" when I speak on race. I've had HR call me their "diversity success story" on Monday, then ignore me on Tuesday when I call something out.

It's not that I don't belong. It's that I'm never allowed to belong fully.

There's always a ceiling. Always a side-eye. Always a question behind the compliment. Always a smile that checks for the edge of your mask.

I've walked into rooms where I was the only one who looked like me. Then walked into other rooms where I was the only one who didn't sound like me. Where do you breathe, when every space takes something from you?

A constant negotiation between how you feel inside and what the world decides you are. And that negotiation?

It doesn't end. It follows you into classrooms. Into interviews. Into relationships. Into police stops. Into parenting. Into therapy.

Into silence. I've spent my whole life being too much of one thing and not enough of the other.

Too Black to blend in. Too white to be believed. Too smart to be dismissed. Too angry to be heard.

So I learned to perform. To code-switch. To adapt.

I changed how I walked in rooms. Smoothed out my voice. Nodded at jokes I didn't get, or didn't think were funny. I studied their rules until I could pass every test.

And it worked. But every version of me I created left another version behind.

Somewhere, I stopped knowing which one was real.

And now I'm unlearning all of it.

Not for your benefit. Not for applause. But because I'm tired of bleeding identity just to be tolerated.

I am not a project.

I am not an example.

I am not a box.

And if that makes you uncomfortable? Good.

Sit in that. Like I've sat in everything else.

I don't live in one world. I live in two. And both of them question my presence.

The white world sees my skin and starts editing the story. The Black world hears my voice and wonders if I belong.

But I am not two halves.I am one whole.

Split, maybe, but not broken.

Tired, yes, but not finished.

I've been boxed. Tokenized. Explained. Dismissed. Decorated. But never seen.

So let me make this clear:

I'm not your checkbox. I'm not your mascot. I'm not your story to sanitize or sell.

I'm me.

Unapologetically. Unedited. Uninvited, sometimes. But undeniable.

You want a box?

Fuck that. I'll build a fire instead.

And if it makes you sweat? Again, good.

Maybe now you'll finally feel the heat we live in every day.

Chapter Fourteen

The Podcast

It started in the smallest room in the house.

Spare bedroom. Beige walls. One window, half-blocked by a blanket I tacked up to kill the echo. Card table from a yard sale. Chair with a crack in the vinyl seat. Nothing fancy.

Just me.

And the mic I bought online, mid-range, nothing pro. Headphones taped. Laptop second hand.

I called the podcast Fuck That before I even recorded the first word.

It wasn't a branding decision. It wasn't clickbait.

It was the phrase that had been living in my chest for twenty years.

Fuck this form.

Fuck this job.

Fuck this mask.

Fuck this version of me I've been handing out just to survive the room.

I didn't have a launch plan. Didn't write a teaser script or design cover art. I opened a blank file, hit record, and started talking.

The first story was small. But it wasn't.

The girl in the bookstore. The smile. The twelve words that cracked something inside me clean open.

You look like you're from the city…

But you sound like you're from the country.

It wasn't meant to hurt. But it rewired everything.

It told me: the world sees your skin first.

And your story second.

If at all.

I told it raw. No edits. No corrections.

I didn't try to make it relatable. I didn't soften the beat. I just said it the way it still lived in my memory, clear, still, and echoing.

And when I finished, I didn't listen back.

I didn't care if the audio was perfect or if I stumbled a little. I saved the file. Clicked upload. Published it.

That was it.

No post. No promo. No announcement.

I wasn't trying to build an audience.

I was trying to breathe.

Trying to speak one truth that hadn't been tampered with, diluted, or rephrased for broader appeal.

This wasn't a strategy. This was survival.

I sat there in the silence after, headphones off, screen still glowing, and let it land.

Not because I thought anyone would listen.

But because for the first time, I had.

I didn't expect anything. Maybe a few listens. A bot or two. Dead air.

But the next morning, the episode had twenty plays. Then fifty. Then a hundred by the end of the week.

Nothing viral. But not invisible, either.

People started messaging me. Colleagues. Old classmates. A former boss, not David, obviously, someone else. They all had the same tone: a mix of surprise and softness.

"Didn't know you felt this way."

"That story hit me hard."

"Thanks for being honest."

Some of them meant it.

Some were performing the same way I had for years, trying to say the right thing so they didn't have to sit in the wrongness too long.

A few said nothing.

Silence. Ghosts. People I used to talk to every day suddenly out of range. No response, no like, no eye contact in the hallway.

I wasn't surprised.

That's the thing about truth, it doesn't just resonate. It rearranges. It forces people to see what they've chosen to ignore.

Rachel listened twice.

Once alone. Then again while I sat next to her.

When it ended, she didn't speak right away.

She reached over, pressed pause, and said, "That's the first time I've heard you say it. Not just explain it. Say it."

I nodded. Didn't trust myself to speak.

She wasn't complimenting the podcast.

She was naming something deeper. The shift. The voice.

This wasn't me playing safe. This wasn't me trying to educate or appease.

This was the unfiltered version. The version I usually buried under tone, context, and strategy.

And somehow, she loved me more for it.

By Episode 3, the numbers had doubled. Then tripled.

I wasn't promoting. Still hadn't built a website. But it didn't matter. Word was spreading, inbox filling with strangers who saw themselves in the cracks.

Black men, mostly. Mixed folks. Kids who'd been called articulate one too many times. Parents raising kids in-between. White women in HR who said they were "doing the work," and wanted me to know I was "so brave."

Brave.

That word kept showing up. Like I'd run into a burning building instead of just telling the truth in my own damn voice.

Some listeners meant it. Others just liked the sound of my pain in their headphones.

The DMs started asking for more. More episodes. More stories. More lessons.

Some wanted healing.

Some wanted homework.

Some wanted proof that they weren't the problem.

That's when the pressure kicked in.

Every topic felt loaded. Every sentence felt like a negotiation between clarity and consequence. I started second-guessing myself again, not in the way I used to when trying to code-switch, but now as someone who'd been made visible.

They were listening.

They were quoting me.

Some were putting my words into slide decks for their company's next DEI meeting. Some were sharing my clips with no context, just vibes. Some were asking for interviews, panels, keynotes.

I hadn't even bought a new mic yet.

And already, I could feel the frame tightening.

Be radical, but digestible.

Be honest, but hopeful.

Be Black, but balanced.

I wasn't even sure who I was talking to anymore.

The ones who got it didn't need the intro.

The ones who needed the intro didn't always stay past the first five minutes.

I sat at the desk one night, mic on, file open, and couldn't speak. Froze.

Not out of fear, out of fatigue.

Because even now, on my ow n platform, in my own voice, I could feel it creeping back in.

That need to be clear. To be clean. To be careful.

And I hated it.

Because this space, this podcast, was supposed to be where the mask came off.

So I didn't record that night.

I closed the file.

And wrote one sentence on a Post-it I stuck to the mic:

Say it like no one's in the room.

Chapter Fifteen

Balance

The email subject line was: "Opportunity to Elevate Voices"

Rachel forwarded it to me with a single line: "You don't have to do this."

It was from a nonprofit I didn't know, local, white-led, suddenly "very committed to equity."

They were hosting a town hall.

Topic: "Bridging the Divide: Race, Identity, and Hope."

Three words that mean absolutely nothing when spoken by people who've never had to live the divide, explain the identity, or cling to hope like a life raft in a system built to drown you.

They wanted me on the panel.

Not to keynote. Not to open. Just... participate.

There'd be a white woman who led a DEI nonprofit, a white man who wrote a book on "racial healing" after two years in seminary, and a South Asian tech CEO who called himself "race-adjacent" and mostly tweeted startup wisdom over Kendrick lyrics. And then me.

They framed it like a gift.

"We've heard your podcast and think your perspective would bring valuable balance to the conversation."

Balance. Translation: edge. Energy. Contrast. The seasoning to their stew of soft progress.

I was the conflict they could schedule. I almost deleted the email.

But I didn't. I stared at it for a while. Thought about all the panels I'd sat through, nodding, clapping, dying inside. Thought about all the spaces where my presence was the performance. My pain, the curriculum. My survival, the takeaway.

Thought about the times I'd softened my words for the sake of the room.

Then I hit reply. "I'm available. Confirm the time."

Rachel saw the draft. She just said, "You're not doing it for them."

I shook my head. "No. I'm doing it for everyone who's ever had to sit on a stage and pretend it wasn't burning."

This wasn't about being heard. This was about not being silenced.

Not this time.

They wanted a Black voice with polish? Fine. They were about to get one with fire.

The green room wasn't green. It was beige. Like everything else in that building: soft walls, safe lighting, no sharp edges. Just enough comfort to say we care, not enough discomfort to suggest we're listening.

I got there ten minutes early.

Everyone else was already there.

The DEI director stood first, white woman, scarf draped just so, smile tight like she practiced it. "Michael, we're so thrilled to have you here."

She said thrilled like it was supposed to mean grateful, but came out sounding more like strategic.

The moderator gave me the rundown. Time limits. No crosstalk. "Try to end your comments with an action step or takeaway."

An action step.

They wanted trauma, TED Talk style: raw enough to be powerful, clean enough to make it to YouTube.

The other panelists nodded along. The "racial reconciliation" guy wore a sports coat over a hoodie. Casual Woke. The South Asian CEO was already on his phone, drafting his own applause tweet before the event even started.

I sat down, didn't shake hands.

The energy shifted, just slightly. They noticed.

I didn't care.

They filled the space with chatter, talking about their last panel, their media kits, who they were meeting with next. I was the only one not performing yet, which made me the most dangerous person in the room.

Then someone said it.

The DEI woman turned to me and asked, "Just so we're aligned, you're going to focus on storytelling, right? Personal narrative?"

It wasn't a question.

It was a request for containment. Please don't burn the house down.

Please keep it lived-experience-level. Please don't bring the data.

Please don't indict us while we're trying.

I smiled.

One of those small, surgical smiles that doesn't reach the eyes.

"I'll speak from my experience," I said.

That was the truth.

What I didn't say was: My experience is the indictment.

The room got quiet again.

And I realized, they weren't afraid of what I might say.

They were afraid I wouldn't say it the way they could handle.

The lights weren't bright. That surprised me.

I always thought the stage would feel hotter, sharper, but it didn't. It felt like every other panel I'd been on. Chairs in a row. Water bottles with no labels. Audience full of cardigans and good intentions. The moderator opened with a land acknowledgment and a joke. People laughed, the polite kind, the "we're warm now" kind.

Then she introduced the panelists, one by one. The reconciliation guy spoke first. Something about "bridging difference through dialogue." Quoted Baldwin. Mispronounced it. Then the DEI woman, talking about her "years of learning and unlearning." She said the word anti-racism like it had a trademark.

Then the CEO. Tech buzzwords dressed up like revolution. "Authentic disruption." "Scalable empathy."

Then it was my turn.

I didn't stand.

Didn't clear my throat.

Didn't thank the organizers.

Didn't smile.

I just leaned into the mic and said:

"Before we talk about bridging the divide, we need to be honest about who built the gap."

The room went still. No shifting. No coughing. No click of pens.

I kept going.

"Every space I've ever been invited into like this, this exact one, in fact, has asked me to share just enough pain to make you feel informed, but not enough to make you feel indicted."

A few heads dropped. Eyes avoided.

"But I'm not here to make you feel comfortable. I'm not here to balance anything. I'm here because this conversation has been curated, and I'm tired of being the decoration."

No one moved.

I paused. Let the silence do its work.

Then I told them what they didn't want to hear:

That inclusion without power is performance.

That visibility without voice is decoration.

That being asked to speak is not the same as being allowed to tell the truth.

"I'm not your storyteller. I'm not your translator. I'm not here to give you closure." Final beat. Clean. Measured.

"I'm just here to tell you the truth, out loud, in a way you can't edit."

And I leaned back in my chair.

No smile. No summary. No bow.

The crowd didn't clap right away.

But I wasn't waiting.

Chapter Sixteen

What I Kept

No one said anything backstage. Not at first.

The DEI director was the first to move, half-smile still stitched to her face, hands clasped like she was praying I'd vanish politely. "Thank you," she said, voice tight. "Very powerful."

I didn't reply.

The reconciliation guy avoided my eyes. The CEO gave me a nod, like we were co-conspirators in something we weren't.

I walked out the side door.

Didn't stay for photos.

Didn't network.

Didn't check the hashtags.

Rachel was waiting in the car.

She didn't say anything at first, either. Just reached across the console and took my hand.

"You okay?" she asked.

"Yeah," I said.

And I was.

Because for the first time, I hadn't explained myself for someone else's benefit.

I hadn't softened the blow.

Hadn't buffered the language.

Hadn't checked the room before I spoke.

I said what needed to be said.

Clearly.

Unapologetically.

Untranslated.

And the world didn't end. That surprised me more than anything.

Because the first time I ever spoke the truth in public, really spoke it, I got punished.

Third grade. Class discussion on culture. I said I didn't feel Black or white. Just... stuck.

The teacher smiled like I'd said something funny.

A kid called me confused.

The principal told me not to say things that might "alienate others." I learned real quick:

Truth makes people uncomfortable.

And when people get uncomfortable, they reach for control.

Back then, I apologized.

Now? I let the discomfort sit.

They didn't cancel me. Didn't drag me. Didn't throw a parade either. The moment just... passed. And in its place was this quiet. Not peace. Not safety. But clarity.

The kind that settles in your chest after you finally stop performing and realize you're still here. Still standing. Still breathing. Still whole.

That's what I kept.

It wasn't a revolution. Just a shift.

The kind that's easy to miss if you're not paying attention. If you're waiting for fireworks, you won't see it. But it was there, in the small things. I stopped overexplaining in meetings. Let the silence land when someone misunderstood me. Didn't fill it with context just to make them comfortable.

I started dressing for myself again.

Stopped calculating my tone before every email. Stopped ending hard truths with smiley faces. At work, people looked at me different. Not with fear. Not with admiration. More like... uncertainty.

Like they didn't know what version of me was going to walk into the room.

I liked that.

Let them wonder.

I said no more often. No to one more panel. No to mentoring someone who just wanted proximity. No to reviewing someone's "anti-racism" blog post for free. I stopped managing white guilt.

Stopped translating my grief into teachable moments. Started cooking more. Sleeping better. Laughing without checking the room first.

Started answering, "How are you?" with "Tired," and letting that be enough.

Rachel noticed.

"You're quieter," she said one night. "Is that good?" I asked.

She smiled. "It's real."

That's what the shift was.

Not louder. Not meaner. Not radical in the way people expect. Just real.

I wasn't trying to be legible anymore.

And in that space, I started to feel something I hadn't felt in a long time.

Not joy. Not peace.

But presence.

A few months later, I got a new role. Bigger title. More money. Same system. First week, someone emailed me about joining the new DEI council. "We'd love your voice in the room." I wrote back one sentence.

"No, thank you."

No explanation. No performance. No polite deferral to signal I still cared. They followed up. Asked again. Framed it as a "leadership opportunity."

I refused. Again. They weren't happy.

I didn't care. I'm not your mascot. I'm not your balance. I'm not your redemption story. I'm done dressing up oppression as opportunity. I said no. And I meant it. That's the fire. Not rage. Not spectacle.

Just... clarity.

I didn't burn it all down. That's what people expect, right? Rage as a wrecking ball. The big dramatic walkout. The final email that leaves them speechless.

But real change?

It's slower. Quieter. More surgical than cinematic.

I didn't quit my job.

Didn't start a foundation.

Didn't write a book deal thread. I just started building something that didn't require me to shrink.

The podcast grew. Not big. Not famous. But steady. Real people. Real stories. No sponsors. No scripts. Just the sound of someone finally saying it out loud. I talked to other folks like me, the in-between ones. The ones who'd checked "Other" their whole life. Who learned how to smile before they spoke. Who knew what it meant to be too much and not enough in the same breath.

They weren't looking for answers. They just wanted to know they weren't alone.

I started writing again. Not for work. Not for panels. Just for me.

Pieces I never shared. Lines that would never trend. But they were honest. And that was the point.

Rachel helped me build a small studio in the garage. Just soundproofing and shelves. A good chair. A better mic. A space with no masks. No panels. No edits. No code-switching.

Just me.

Telling the truth. One story at a time.

But, not everyone got it. Some coworkers pulled away. A few friends stopped reaching out.

Even on the podcast, some episodes sat quiet. Too raw, too honest. But I didn't care.

Because for the first time, I wasn't chasing impact.

I was documenting existence. Not for them. For me.

For the version of me that used to rehearse every sentence in his head before speaking.

For the kid who thought he had to earn his place by shrinking.

This was for him.

Proof that you can speak plainly. Breathe fully. Live wholly.

Not without consequence. But without shame.

Chapter Seventeen

No Apologies

I'm an introvert. Always have been.

I grew up avoiding confrontation like it was a trap.

Taught myself how to shrink in a room, how to disappear without leaving.

Don't make a scene.

Don't stir the waters.

Keep it quiet. Keep it clean.

But here's the problem with that:

Everyone learns it.

And when everyone stays quiet, nothing shifts.

I waited. Watched. Hoped someone louder, braver, more certain would step in.

But there weren't enough voices. Not really.

And that's not how real change shows up.

Real change is someone saying no and meaning it.

Real change is someone speaking plainly and not apologizing for the echo.

Real change is not needing their reaction to validate your truth.

I used to think I had to be calm to be heard.

But rage isn't the enemy.

Rage is the truth unmuted.

Rage is clarity.

Rage is earned.

And I'm done apologizing for it.

I'm done folding myself into shapes they can process.

Done explaining my tone.

Done waiting for permission to speak.

They wanted the safe version.

They got the mirror.

I stopped explaining.

Stopped translating.

Stopped trying to sound like someone they'd invite to brunch after the panel.

The people who love the status quo?

They're counting on our silence.

They've made an art of fear. Taught us that to speak is to risk.

They know we believe that silence is complicity.

So they make sure we stay silent.

But someone has to break that.

I didn't think it would be me.

It wasn't a spark.

It was subtraction.

Less performing. Less buffering.

More space to breathe.

People keep asking what changed.

Like they missed it.

Like there was a single moment, a clean break, a headline that marked the shift.

There wasn't.

No protest. No resignation. No viral clip.

Just a quiet decision:

Stop folding.

Stop softening.

Stop making myself easy to hold.

So here I am.

Not marching.

Not giving keynotes.

Just writing and talking.

And that's enough.

Because words move.

Words burn.

And I've bled enough for these.

I'm going to use them.

My son asked me once why I started the podcast.

We were sitting at the kitchen table. Sunday morning. Cereal bowls half full. He was old enough to notice things now. The weight behind my voice. he shape of the words I didn't say.

I didn't give him the long version. Didn't talk about the HR meetings or the panels or the silence that made me bite my tongue for years. I just said: "Because I got tired of pretending."

He nodded. Didn't ask for more.

And I knew that he understood something deeper than the words,

That his father used to be quiet out of fear,

and now wasn't quiet at all.

That matters.

Because one day, someone will try to box him too.

They'll look at his skin and decide what he's allowed to be.

They'll ask him to soften. To explain. To shrink.

And he'll have to choose.

But he won't have to do it alone.

He'll have my voice in his ear.

My words in the air.

Not as rules.

Not as a burden.

As presence.

Something to carry.

Something to light the way.

Because I wasn't put here to be palatable.

I was put here to be true.

To be whole. To be heard.

Because the truth is:

We are not a checkbox.

Not on your form.

Not in your system.

Not in your story.

We are not your diversity win.

Not your teachable moment.

Not your favorite exception.

We are complicated. Conflicted. Still angry. Still learning. Still here.

You don't have to understand that.

But you damn sure don't get to define it.

I've spent most of my life being asked to define myself in terms someone else could understand.

Pick a side.

Check a box.

Be clear. Be consistent. Be easy to explain.

And for a long time, I tried.

I played the role.

Wore the masks.

Perfected the voice.

I made myself legible, one setting at a time.

Black enough to be trusted.

White enough to be safe.

Angry enough to seem aware.

Soft enough not to scare anyone.

I was never lying.

I was just editing.

Every day, a new draft of me, shaped by rooms that didn't want the truth...

They wanted the version that kept things moving.

The version they could put on a flyer and feel good about.

But the truth doesn't care about flyers.

The truth is: I'm not white.

The truth is: I don't fit.

The truth is: I've been treated like a threat and a token, often in the same breath.

And I'm done asking for permission to say that out loud.

I wasn't put here to be palatable.

I was put here to burn what needed burning,

And leave behind something brighter.

Not perfect.

But real.

I am not quiet anymore.

I am not a mascot.

And this is not a rant.

It's a reclamation.

Of voice.

Of self.

Of every moment I was asked to shrink and stayed quiet.

So remember this:

I don't need your labels.

I don't need your comfort.

I need this:

No translations.

No edits.

No apologies.

Chapter Eighteen

Epilogue

If you read this and thought, "He's mad," my question is: Why aren't you?

Why are you still quiet?

You know what a silent protest is? An excuse to be ignored.

Stop worrying about what people are going to say about you, and start worrying about what you're going to say to your kids when they ask why you didn't fight back. Why you didn't speak up. Why you cared more about how people saw you than what they did to you.

Change is never made passively.

Even the great Reverend Dr. Martin Luther King, Jr., a pacifist, moved millions of people to act. Was he peaceful? Yes. Was he quiet? No.

There's a difference.

I'm not telling you to be reckless. I'm not telling you to be violent. I'm telling you to stop rolling over.

Look at yourself in the mirror. Speak your truth. In the only way you can.

And if you hear that old lie, "What can I do? I'm just one person,", remember this:

Every movement is made of individuals. Every spark starts as a single flame.

You don't have to lead a march. You don't have to have a platform. But you do have a voice.

Use it.

And if you can't use it yet? Then be the reason someone else does.

Be the motivation.

Be the match.

About the Author

Joshua Ericson is a mixed-race writer, speaker, and technology leader based in Connecticut.

He writes about mental health, identity, and the lifelong pressure to perform in spaces never designed for truth. His work blends personal experience with cultural critique, challenging readers to confront what too often goes unspoken.

His debut book, *Think, Rethink, Panic*, chronicled his journey through anxiety, therapy, and radical self-awareness. *Fuck That* is something different, rawer, sharper, and louder. It's the moment the mask cracked, and the voice underneath finally came through unfiltered.

When he's not writing, Joshua builds things, software, stories, furniture, or a life that doesn't require translation.

He lives in Connecticut with his wife, kids, and more ideas than time.

"Not professionally approved, but emotionally accurate."